Icarus Doe is an American writer, entrepreneur, active volunteer, and travel enthusiast. She is a semi-retired business consultant, gardener, and lover of travel. It is this entrepreneurial spirit and her grit of business that inspire her to write stories about women who live in patriarchal societies, with little monetary equality and repressed sexuality.

To all the Ninas I have met in this life. May the wind lift
your lust and pursuit for equality.

Icarus Doe

DILDO-GATE II

Chasing Tail

AUSTIN MACAULEY PUBLISHERS®

LONDON ● CAMBRIDGE ● NEW YORK ● SHARJAH

Ordering Information
Quantity sales: Special discounts are available on quantity purchases by corporations, associations, and others. For details, contact the publisher at the address below.

Publisher's Cataloging-in-Publication data
Doe, Icarus
Dildo-Gate II

ISBN 9798891554306 (Paperback)
ISBN 9798891554313 (ePub e-book)

Library of Congress Control Number: 2023905398

www.austinmacauley.com/us

First Published 2024
Austin Macauley Publishers LLC
40 Wall Street, 33rd Floor, Suite 3302
New York, NY 10005
USA

mail-usa@austinmacauley.com
+1 (646) 5125767

Table of Contents

Prologue   9

Chapter 1: 1970s   12

Chapter 2: The Jubilee   18

Chapter 3: The Return Trip   24

Chapter 4: In Route   28

Chapter 5: Touring   33

Chapter 6: Dinner   41

Chapter 7: Last Night   43

Chapter 8: Cottages   48

Chapter 9: Ghosted   52

Chapter 10: The Dream   57

Prologue

The Jenga puzzle continues. A story of our traveler, Andrea, her sexuality, and a deep sense of place intertwined with thematic adventures and a tense political backdrop of Eastern Europe.

It is a relief to touchdown, the 9,000 km flight and her return from Eastern Europe were uneventful and cramped, much like Andrea's mind. Returning home, unpacking methodically, and rehashing Ahmed's harsh words – the peculiar interchange and rejection. Scowling at the thought of Irina, her midnight tryst with Ahmed, and her son's tragic death on the holy Georgia's Day of the Dead – hapless suicide. She loathes Irina.

Thinking of beautiful Nina and hoping they will always be friends. Will Ahmed shun Andrea away like others? And Nina's dispensing of the vibrators expeditiously with some profit – batteries not included – sanitized in petite gift boxes.

Med safely returns to his home somewhere in Turkey. Her cappuccino lover promises a new rendezvous in Europe and a visit to his home.

Weeks fade into a month, then two, with message emojis from Ahmed indicating prayer and the celebration of

Easter, hints of forgiveness, and the future. Andrea ignores his offers. She places her matching Claddagh ring inside the box on her dresser in her dream cottage.

The war in Ukraine wages on, NATO allies mounting billions in support, supplying munitions, planes, bombs, and drones. Landmines intermittently detonate on the shores of the Black Sea, a thousand miles south of Sebastopol. The very spot where her tale takes place. Egypt is pressed for food as the dollar crashes. The UAE is positioning to see if its interests are met and the Saudis are trading oil without using the $. China and Taiwan relations are at a new low and Russia's ruler Putin loosely speaks about using the nuclear bomb as Zelensky counts on a Western-backed offense.

Post-COVID-19, America continues its path of division, ex-president Trump is not many steps from a jail or bankruptcy, and the country is on the edge of civil turmoil. Should Trump flee America and rule remotely? much like Georgia's former President Mikheil Saakashvili? Ultimately captured, to be captured, subsequently tortured and left starving in the modern gulag. Fallout from the Supreme Court ruling on Roe v. Wade; states are restricting abortions, and morning-after pills are next, then all contraception.

The exodus of refugee families, journalists, and war dodgers continues to Georgia, the smallest of countries geopolitically pressed throughout history. The understated Silk Road crossing. New draft restrictions in Russia send thousands more to neighboring Georgia with bags of rubles. Daily, people stream across the borders of Eastern Europe and Turkey. With a population under 4 million, tiny Georgia appeases Russia they need gas and wheat.

Stories of a vibrant economy from the bribes at mountainous Russian/Georgian border crossings to the rumors that five kilos of potatoes buy a vote easily – a simple ballot stuffing.

Fear of a secondary war front, sense of rigged voting, and the party in power being pro-Russian thus, corrupt. Hundreds of thousands take to the streets of Tbilisi decrying the government's crackdown on foreign investment in civil society and a path toward the European Union.

Allegiance contracts are demanded by hotels and bars denouncing Russia. Graffiti scrawls and images of "Fuck Russia" painted on overpasses and seaside billboards. Russians fill both the capital city and Black Sea hotels. Overstaying their welcome, bringing their chichi dogs on leashes, and stepping over the locally scattered stray dogs.

Chapter 1
1970s

She ignores the endless WhatsApp messages from Guadalajara. A Ken doll from her past. There are too many. Sexting relentlessly with dick pics.

Med, Andrea's Turkish lover, is messaging too, wanting Andrea to join him in London, it is spring, and the Queen's Jubilee.

"My beautiful lady, please come. My work takes me there."

Andrea: "We'll see."

"Wear a white bra, I will make love to your ass. You will scream."

She thinks about his scent and thinks it daunting to return to flight so soon, but softens from his cry for a company in his messages, meeting will quench her growing thirst.

"Okay, I'll come, but only for a few days." She types while remunerating in her mind, *My ass? What's with men and their ass fetish?* So many synonyms for ass; orifice, bunghole, muscles sphincter, ani porta, arse, arsehole, asshole, sphincter ani, rectum, imperforate anus, opening.

And slang for men: boy cunt, boy pussy, corn hole. Plenty of names, interestingly enough.

But right now, rest is what Andrea needs. She retreats to her bedroom, silences her Android, lays her head on a soft pillow, looks at the ceiling, and meditates.

Andrea returns to her youth, a vivid memory of the spring of '75, a time of short skirts, platform shoes, bell bottoms, and headbands with peace signs embroidered onto handbags and jeans. Silver metal wristbands stamped with 'MIA' and accented with red, white, and blue sticker stars. Youth's message of hope for unaccounted soldiers, after the fall of Saigon ending the war in Vietnam and post-Watergate.

It's Andrea's last year of Catholic school, 8th grade. Strict nuns with habits and rules upon rules, plus guilt. Vatican II in the 1960s relaxed the dress habit – a nun's uniform. Remaining humble and plain; all black with an accent of white trim at the collar and veil. Gone are the long, flowing, full black garments depicted in *The Handmaid's Tale*. And the matching long black veil with an inner white lining and a tall papal starched cap. Only hands are exposed. Their shoes, a black militaristic boots, oddly popular in the twenty-first century empowering army wear. Nuns towered over small children even if short. The shyest small children would urinate in their seats, rather than request an extra visit to the lavatories at strictly assigned times. Where, in 8th grade, students are granted the privilege to raise their hand and request to be excused for the lavatory, a rarely heard noun nowadays.

It was the year amidst the streak fad when young men dropped their pants and dashed across the playing field at

Shea Stadium in Queens, New York. Hairy balls and phalluses swing freely as the pigs run chase. It was the same year her classmate, John, did the same.

Brown lunch bag packed by stay-at-home moms for half-hour recess. Lanky John, his voice just breaking, flaunted brown, flaxen loose hair that reached his shoulders, ironed navy pants, and a white shirt with a Snap-On blue tie. On a dare, playing ball in the boys' field, John loosens his brown belt and drops his pants. Free in public, he makes a dash fully hung, with a full bush, methodically flapping phallus, slapping each side of his thigh, with his gait.

Andrea missed seeing these details as boys and girls were separated in the school playing fields. But all her classmates listened to the pastor's lecture on sinning, all seem bizarre and confused. She had no brothers. Just a denuded Ken doll at her cousin's house.

At pajama parties, girls did share secrets. Overnight sleepovers of a dozen or so young ladies to celebrate birthdays were common; a painted palace and a pony ride at the farm were dreams for rich girls. Moms made the cake and the girls piled in blankets and pillows and retreated to the unfinished basements.

In circles chattering, "Should they dare make out with boys? Or admit they passed first base?" and discerning, "Does kissing make you have a baby?" Pleasures were sneaking in boys to spin the bottle, a candle-lit séance, and truth or dare – hot games. Play 45s to rock pop heartthrobs and chant girls' rhymes with arms swinging. Only thought of real kisses made her the girls chant,

"We must, we must, we must increase our bust. the bigger the better the tighter the sweater!"

We are all outgrowing our pretend Kens dolls and knew we were at the precipice of true lust.

Andrea's early passion for shoes began during this time, in grade school. Wrapped in plaid uniforms, only shoes could distinguish any uniqueness, possibly socks, but those were knee-high and regulated to blue or dark green. The homogenous regiment of uniforms assisted with an order, eliminating social status, as students dressed exactly the same.

Plaid skirts, regularly checked for length, bow ties yellow man shirts with Peter Pan collars buttoned up. The nuns ran routine drills lining up the girls as early as 5th grade. The boys were escorted out of the room. Sister Rose, her measuring stick in hand methodically, slowly inspected. Shoes were examined and from your knee to the edge of your skirt for no more than one inch above the knee, if not, you were returned home for mothers to promptly lengthen your skirt hem. Should you be wearing your shiny black patent leather Sunday shoe that was another reason to be sent home. Boys look up your skirt from the reflection and glance at your white lollipop brand undergarment.

It was near Easter time and white shoes were allowed and an Easter dress. Saving quarters from cleaning bikes or gifts from her nana, while shopping, spies a pair of platform white patent leather shoes, with two broad straps; sandal style, and a silver buckle clasp. Then her first mini dress, not too short under her mother's watch. The dress was a shirt dress of flowing nylon, brown with blended pink and peach old-fashioned roses, green leaves, and a matching nylon string belt.

One Sunday the weather was glorious and a Catholic confirmation ceremony was planned mid-day with picnic celebrations after. Andrea chooses the new dress and shoes for a walk with friends. She passed her mother's inspection, only her top button was open, and little did it matter because her breasts were just developing – plum size. A white lace trim slip underneath and new beige big girl stockings.

Walking was common in the 70s, no two and four-car garages. Andrea grew up in the post-WWII; with a starter monopoly house and packed neighbors and kids – baby boomers. A one-family car is considered normal and anything within a few miles or even ten miles of one's home could be accomplished by foot or bike. Post WII expansion of suburbs provided little or no bus or train transit, except in the town center.

Andrea and her friends meet at the corner near her home, they walk down the hill for ten minutes, take a left at the bottom, and meander along the narrow tree-lined tarred road to the church. Giggling freely as girls do. Strolling and chatting. A car comes alongside with yelling boys, one reaches out and explicitly yells "Gotcha!" and slaps her ass hard as they speed away. Stunned, an odd warm feeling as if she is playing with Ken and Barbie. She says nothing, her first real sensual response to aggression.

Awakened, hours passed, she'd slept long enough, and it's time to regenerate her routine of preen, plump, and reviving – readying for London. She sets a string of appointments; hair, facial, massage. Her Botox is still fresh.

Ping! It is Nina. "And when will you come again?"

Andrea: "First London then just after we will talk, should be able to squeeze it in." Continuing. "Nina, yes I will return. And two lady guests, we will need to tour with them." Andrea had made promises to visit her other friends and visit Georgia. Now, without COVID restrictions, some tension over international travel were simplified. Uneasy, but determined to keep her promises to friends.

Nina: "Good, send the plane tickets, and their passport copies to confirm the exact dates."

Med: "We will meet at Kings Cross, my train from New Castle arrives at noon. We will spend all day together. You will wear black high heels a black short skirt, a white bra, and thong and a white silk shirt. Then I will lick the wetness between your legs. And I am short on money, do you have $1,000?"

Seeing the money request, Andrea's heart sank. "I will arrive at Heathrow earlier in the day. Then Uber to Kings Cross, it will take about an hour in traffic. From there, we can take the tube to the center and check-in. Be an animal when we close our door." She types while ignoring Med's request for money.

Chapter 2
The Jubilee

The UK is a short trip and an easy pack. US–UK relations are good and the borders recently opened. Only a European-sized carry-on roller bag is sufficient, an eight kg weight limit on board. Just the minimum two pants, requested undergarments all sexy, four pairs of socks, extra shoes, four tops, makeup, creams, shampoo, and perfume all small-sized. Yes, snacks, dried rehydration crystals, a small stock of medicines, and warming lube, if necessary. Andrea has a hacking cough, so she takes a COVID test and is relieved it is negative. Unlike in Eastern Europe flights, the border police rarely check cash in transit routing to London for the solo traveler.

The coach flight was a whopping $1,600 Jubilee price and $300 for any hotel abutting Hyde Park, no first-class budget this trip, and Med is short on cash apparently. Boarding was unusually smooth and the flight was relatively short.

Andrea's blue carry-on slips easily in the overhead bin with priority boarding. Her petite pink Coach purse slung around her neck and tucked into its side pocket $1,000 additional cash. She picks at her drab plane food, has an uneventful deep sleep, curled in her favorite aisle seat number ten on a coach flight. Neither close to the toilet nor the bulkhead with kids, yet prompt drinks and food service.

After a soft landing and waking up, her cough persists and worsens. She shrugs over the thought of handing out money, not even caring about the reason; men lie about why money is needed.

Andrea wonders if she is like *Helen Miren's* role in *The Roman Spring of Mrs. Stone* (2003). A post-war tale that takes place in Rome, the economy is in full collapse. Mrs. Stone, a suddenly widowed actress past her prime, is befriended by an Italian countess selling gigolos to make ends meet. The rendezvous fills her sorrow with lust. A fading actress past her prime hooked on the coupling to quell the pain of loss and aging, affirming her youth. She drafts checks to her lovers with an empty expression. No, Andrea is too confident.

Off boarding at Heathrow, Andrea is on the Jetway. Borders recently opened, Heathrow is crowded like an exotic zoo. A chaotic snake-line presents itself with hundreds of tired confused travelers, crying children in tow, beyond maximum carry-on pieces tied to backs and slung in arms in a haphazard manner. Pushing, shimmying aggressively, and clamoring in all languages. A bustling madhouse.

Like a spring river, Andrea is part of the flow, with logs, sticks, and boulders to navigate. Like the spring salmon upstream seeking to breed. The queue forms a secondary queue with signs pointing Americans the right and other passports to "this way." In a new queue, each traveler can choose passport agents or the machine. Forty-five minutes pass and she picks the automated passport machine. 2 hours remain for a timely rendezvous at Kings Crossing.

Her turn is next, she opens her passport but it won't lie flat easily. The machine fails. Then again, it fails. Again and again. Looking behind her, the long line is doubled for machine entry, yet triple the length to visit a live agent. Spying on an adjacent machine, she cuts the front of the queue to the right and shoves her flattened passport, easily slipping through.

The UK just reopened its borders and the two-year backlog of visitors and the Jubilee created mayhem; a people tsunami. Escalators and elevators are backlogged with confused travelers. Signs were confusing and sparse. The glory of 2012 London is gone; London is stripped bare in appearance by Covid restrictions.

Short of words and now exhausted, Andrea is pointed to a lift and the second floor, her Uber platform. No hope of getting the lift anytime soon. Another hour passed. She locates a less crowded line that ascends one floor, then anxiously exits to a circular platform with fat columns, in a covered garage.

Greeted by more chaos, fewer signs, beeping, and travelers with checked luggage. A friendly enough traffic attendant points at the sidewalk. "To the right 4th column. Hail Uber from that spot." She does and it arrives.

Descending, traffic out of the winding garage and airport was close to an hour. She types: "On my way, just late."

Med: "No worries, I am at the cafe with the red awning on the second floor."

Her coughing persists, deepening. She'll be careful to not mix the names Ahmed and Med.

Relieved, the ride to Kings Cross is calming, the rolling row houses, decent spring weather, winding highways, and soft-spoken driver; perfect. Arriving and exiting the car, Andrea looks forward, crowds persist and she enters the grand hall. It is her first look at glorious arched ceilings made of arcing iron and transparent glass mirroring the great medieval cathedrals; ecclesiastical. Gazing up, the red awning is easy to spot. One more inquiry to a stranger who points to the escalator. "Hello, Med."

Med says nodding, "You really came."

Grinning, she says, "Why yes indeed!" He looked tan, his smile so white. Softly, they whisper and catch up with each other over coffee. "Dear, you must know I am sick with a cough," she says. Andrea likes this Ken doll, he understands and responds calmly.

After navigating the tube and a walk, they arrive at the check-in. The receptionist giggles easily seeing the 20-year age gap. They scurry towards the elevator, embrace deeply then kiss, exit the elevator, locate their room, and lock the door behind them. A doctor of chemistry, he created a lubricant gel, a gift. Both pleased, they tear at each other's clothes, only Andrea's thong remains.

"Ouch!" It is not like the last tryst. Med pushes and turns her towards the wall, and repletely paddles her buttocks. He reaches around and squeezes her plump breasts. "Oh, yes," she whispers. His penis erects with the warm lube he used. He massages her breast with one hand and separates her legs with the other, moving her thong to one side. He lifts his hand from her breast and places it at the small of her back to bend her back forward. Submitting willingly, she leans. With the same hand, he fingers her gently testing for wetness and shoving a second then third finger deep into her. Progressing, she moans as his thumb is thrust into her anus. As she screams, he stops, then begins again with his erection thrusting into her wet vagina, then anus, holding her by the back of her neck. She cries, "Stop!" He pleasures only himself; she submits telling her he loves her. Throws her to the bed demanding fellatio. Pulling and grabbing her curly long dark hair toward his groin.

Pumping his erect penis in her mouth she gags as he pulls out and cums on her breast. Quiet tears, and no pleasure.

Oddly, she is aroused after he finishes, he places his hands on her clitoris, and she reaches orgasm as he rubs her unlovingly. They order food and it arrives; hamburgers. He watches as Andrea slowly eats.

Med stares into her eyes and tells her a long tale. His eyes are wild and he is speaking each detail in broken English. "I think my wife was cheating. I ask her and she says no. I put the tracking software on her phone and followed her. I knew this man and asked him if this sex with my wife was true. He says no. I catch them both fucking on the office table. I hate her so much. I want to kill her very badly. Yes, kill her. You cannot divorce in my culture, there are children, and I do not want sex with her!"

Knowing this tale resonates with the truth, Andrea thinks of self-preservation. "Oh, so sad about this. Let's enjoy London and the celebration, tomorrow we will walk." Her appetite is now stifled. Her night is filled with relentless coughing; dismissing this dreaded tale and rough sex.

The morning follows and calm sets in, together they walk hand in hand through Hyde Park, view the changing of the guards, ride the London Eye overlooking the Thames, and are in awe at Buckingham Palace and the Tower of London. Throngs of jubilant onlookers from all corners of the world. British flags hoisted high atop towering poles. A passerby pauses them and offers to photograph the moment with the Eye in the background. Ironic, as if they are newlyweds.

Returning to their room, Andrea is aroused from the day's adventures and wants what she came for. She nibbles on his chest and dominates him, climaxing willingly on him. She masturbates his penis so he cums deeply. Both rest into a deep sleep.

Awakening, she whispers, love drunk from the calming effects, "Med dear, is faithfulness an expectation?"

He replies, "No, this is natural."

She let out a sigh of relief while keeping her now locked phone in sight.

Med whispers, "Do you remember the $1,000?" Taking money in his hand, he leaves quietly thanking Andrea only later, but implores her to visit the doctor. Her cough was now wretched.

The return from Heathrow is less hectic, Andrea seeks treatment for her cough again testing negative for COVID-19, but endures weeks of coughing eventually subsides with antibiotics. Pondering is she Typhoid Mary? Her 100th test with extensive travel the past two years, all negative. Even with no restrictions, the test made sense. Typhoid Mary was a 19th cook who was claimed to have infected up to 122 people with Typhoid in her life, never actually contracting the disease herself.

Chapter 3
The Return Trip

Andrea curiously asks, "And, Nina, what of this Irina? And the vibrators?"

"Oh, she has been gone for months, and vibrators are all sold, we can now get them from China."

"Good, dear, one less problem and you are so right about this Irina." Andrea ponders if this is true.

Knowing of her return, tensions had softened between her and Ahmed and she is thinking of returning her Claddagh ring to her finger. He pings back on Andrea's question as if listening in on her and Nina. "This Irina, I owe her nothing, she is still in the mountains. When will these friends with yours come?" He continues. "Are you investing in the cottages?"

"Soon we start, we are buying the land. The plan is $25,000." The once-claimed love Irina is now disposed of and Andrea ponders again, *Ken dolls lie.*

Her heart cringes reflecting on her dream; the cottages in the canyon; to wear her ring again and both her and Ahmed together. But only a similar end; dumped like Irina like the multi-use vibrators.

Changing the topic she asks, "Set of vibrators?"

"Not needed," he says, "we need knives and remember the vitamins and find this gel enhancer for my manhood, no pills please only enhancing gel and pistachios, chocolate, and..."

Andrea asks jokingly, "Knives?"

"Ass plugs, Interested?"

She texts Ahmed, sending him a link to the Amazing Intimacy store. Ahmed texts back a smiley face. He promptly chooses 'Mistress backdoor butt, please' with an image attached to avoid confusion. She silently contemplated why this butt fetish. She texts him again.

"Ahmed, is anal penetration homosexual?"

"No dear, means more desire for tightness." As years pass, her vulva admittedly stretched from childbirth, but surgery on this is a definite no. Ahmed says, "You should trim your bush more, you're a big girl."

Grumbling internally, she replies, "We will continue later, dear." She drafts a list of travel cargo.

Andrea makes a last-minute trip to the intimacy store and fills her bag with the recommended gel and male enhancement staying power from new clerk who is an approachable gay man with a good toy and enhancing knowledge. So very pleasant, so upbeat; a coiffed appearance. Strolling, she spies a petite butt plug on sale; it is shaped like a small plum fruit but narrow on the end. The cap or plug handle is embellished with a crystal-shaped heart, a gift, a surprise for Nina or maybe herself; stimulating butt training. The check-out clerk confirms it is cute too. CVS has an intimacy section; they have wised up to customer demand and all packaging is discrete with descriptions, items are plainly displayed, unlike the modern kink Intimacy store.

Then she pans eBay for Henkel knives. Individual ones, not group packs as those have missing items or these packs have items not wanted. Henkel's are the best. She is wary that she'll accidentally select an unbranded knock-off. Hand-wrought steel heated then hammered, making a razor's edge; different sizing for butchering meat from the bone, pairing fruit's delicate skin, or dicing and slicing vegetables paper thin if needed. Sharp, long, and sturdy. Selecting new ones not used, she orders three; they should arrive well before her flight.

This trip is a light packing routine for this shorter touring visit. Again, a challenge to read through custom restrictions. She decides to delay reading and only packs chocolate and nuts. Certainly; the butt plug falls under immoral material. An English translation is often poor, thus re-reading custom restrictions is a slog: rules state no knives and immoral goods. Bold from her last trip she simply packs the Henkel knives and anal plug and gel, it is only a gift not an import for trade or a weapon. However, the bold back door rubber Mistress helper stays stateside at Amazing Intimacy, this would be noticed, then taken to the same place the dildos now live.

Giggling, Andrea envisions the rubber model propped in doggie style with melon round cheeks, pink anal and vaginal openings. Her Ken dolls place it against the chair or bed; erect themselves to hump, then repeat. A reusable partner with a quick soaping. Intimacy stores sell a special soap for such toys and on closely reading lubricant gel labels, most state they are not harmful for ingestion.

Mistress Backdoor Butt is almost as good as a glory hole; a slot in a wall in which a man inserts his penis and sexually receives stimulation on the other side from a person; for a hefty payment, of course! A glory hole as depicted in the 2007 film *Irina Palm*. Where a middle-aged grandmother works in a sex club desperately seeking money for her grandson's life-saving surgery, even developing tennis elbow. As an unskilled laborer, well paid work choices are limited.

Irina's arm eventually ends up in a sling, and one afternoon at a ladies luncheon, Irina shares her tale as to why her arm is laid up. Frankly explaining she jerks off men through a glory hole. Her lady's lunch companions gasp deeply, yet listen intently. Andrea digresses, thinking there is no such thing as a sex club for ladies, at least to her knowledge. There were diddler doctors in the 1800s for hysteria treatment, a common diagnosis for women.

Hysteria, a 2011 film, depicts the hilarity of lines of women lining up at doctor diddler, as his massage methodology produces paroxysmal convulsions to treat the disorder "hysteria." An actual medical condition during Victorian times that presented as exaggerated emotional behavior of women with no underlying scientific cause for symptoms. In the lead role, the doctor invents a vibrator from a modified electric duster; as he suffers acute hand and wrist cramping from the booming business. A trial occurs, where hysteria is thought of and treated as a mental illness necessitating patient asylum. The device makes the doctor rich and greatly increases women's satisfaction. At trial, he explains hysteria is not a disease, but a woman's desire from a lack of sexual fulfillment at home from unloving partners.

Chapter 4
In Route

Her routine begins with hair, nails, facial, and massage, the flight is long. Pink sparkle gel with tips this trip. Her guests agree on JFK as the departure from the city. Andrea's energy is high, she will share all the details she loves of Eastern Europe. The food, the eclectic architecture, gondolas, waterfalls, canyons, and caves. We limousine to the airport and hours before departure, they'll comfortably visit the elite lounges at JFK and sample the sprawling new mall at Istanbul International Airport.

One last item before the flight. Andrea reaches into her jewelry box and places the Claddagh ring back on.

Arrival at the airport is timely and so is boarding. However, the plane is queued for two hours on the tarmac and the ventilation is poor and stifling; only at near take-off is water offered. Andrea's blood vessels in her ankles broke and swelled. Disney rash before the ten-hour flight to Istanbul. It will take a week for them to heal. Her seat is deliberately separate from her lady friends, she snores and prefers the coach aisle near if not row ten, if not first-class aisle, then a maximum of two seats. Not the bulkhead area, which is small for overseas flights and will likely have small children in the row. Andrea's inside window seat is taken by a middle-aged handsome Lebanese man. He feels her excitement and strikes up a conversation; it's a transatlantic flight.

This potential Ken Doll was flirtatious and chatty, tall and a dark beauty. The conversation turns personal quickly, she was wearing her bustier for back support and her cleavage was rich. She sees him gazing intermittently. He reveals he is divorced, rebounding from a cheating ex-wife who clubbed at night blowing many men in the working town they lived in. He cuts hair for a living and his ex-wife enjoys a vibrator and he loves to make her happy.

Andrea is familiar with such offbeat conversations as a single traveler seated on a plane. The tight seats are akin to a confessional and one stranger shares secrets; atoning. This chat is very odd.

He offers his shoulder for Andrea's head, lifting the armrest. Begins to caress her knee and close his eyes. Slowly moving his hands slowly up her leg, then down, leaning his head further into her. Feeling aroused, she allowed it for hours, touching his hand intermittently. She thinks he'll follow her to the toilet for mile-high love or respond by touching his groin, but she holds back. Instead, placing the armrest down, he retreats to the back of the plane to sleep only to return when attendants move him back up. No more small talk occurred. He provided his name, but it is already forgotten. Air travel has its oddities and like the boys slapping her ass in grade school that summer or Med having his way, she did not alert an attendant. The goal is the trip, not hours in security at the switch in Istanbul. A 70s generation flaw; bear the advances, do not speak up.

Ahmed texts, "On your way?"

Andrea: "Just at the switch."

"Nina will greet you at the airport and how are my goods, Andrea?"

Andrea quips, "Well cared for, as usual."

"Well, you will all visit the canyon and we can talk." Andrea replies, "Yes, and the caves. What will we talk about?" No response.

Med texts, "Where are you? I will come again, it is so very close."

Andrea replies, "Okay."

Landing safely, Nina greets her. "Good to see you, dear."

"Yes indeed, allow me to introduce my long-time friends, Missy and Lori. We only had a small issue at passport control, they demanded our boarding pass, Missy misplaced hers, but fortunately located it. We were then stopped at the border baggage control. But when responding in the local dialect, the guard waves us on with a smile, thanking us graciously!" Andrea was privately relieved the knives, nuts, candy, butt plug, and gel were safely crossed and cash under the $10,000 limit are intact.

Unpacking and settling in, Andrea hands Nina a small chocolate. "Take these pistachios to Ahmed."

"A peace offering?"

"Yes, you must." The tension had not dissipated from the last visit.

Nervously, Nina says, "Fine, no problem." At the room, all the guests settled in.

Nina visits Andrea privately in her room.

More relaxed from the long flight, Nina and Andrea return to girl talk. It seemed the right time to pass along her gifts. Deep in conversation, discussing bad lovers and good lovers. Getting stood up and standing up well-deserving jerks. They chime together, "With a good vibrator you do not need a bad lover." Resoundingly pleased with her purple choice lipstick shape vibrator with nubs from the last visit.

Andrea smiles broadly. "Maybe this will interest you?"

Nina asks, "What is this you talk about?"

"Anal stimulator for women, let me look, I know it's packed."

Nina asks, "Is it your only one?"

"Yes, but it's simple to get another." Fumbling through the luggage, she opens the unused eyeglass case it was packed in with a lint wipe. "Nina, take it, it's never used."

Nine says, smiling back, "I love it!"

"Good!" Both blushing, they hug.

"I love the eyeglass case!"

"Oh, keep this too, I hardly ever use it and it is so discreet!"

The eyeglass case was a find in a Floridian give shop; hard-cased rounded sides oval with a tropical motif and coordinating blue handles; a mini purse for your best eyewear. Rarely, if ever, used; Andrea's pink purse and most of her purses were too petite to carry this case as it is.

"Andrea, hold it, please."

Andrea responds, "No prob." Although Nina boldly presents herself, she possesses a cultural shyness. She must not be caught by her mother as she lives with her mother happily. A shame of mom knowing or a shame of being caught with masturbation toys. She wants to experiment to titillate and explore herself. The case made it so discreet and fun. It was days later on an errand with other lady colleagues when Andrea passed along the eyeglass case to Nina in the car, saying, "You forgot your glasses!"

Chapter 5
Touring

Her friends visit Andrea's favorite salon. Missy and Andrea have an appointment for half US price Botox and Lori has a massage. Andrea needs to update her gel nails as they are chipped in transit.

Andrea checks in on her to find she is covered in numbing cream. Missy is talked into hundreds of hydraulic acid injections. Excruciating stabs to her face over an hour. Worried, she texts Nina photos of the bottle label, it's in Russian! The clinician is Russian too. Relieved, Missy survives, swollen face, black and blue as if bitten by bees.

Andrea's manicurist is Russian. Her mousy brown hair and brilliant green eyes tell of her escape from Moscow. Softly she mumbles, "A manicurist finds work in a day and her husband works on computers, no children both near age 30 or more; all her friends are waiting to have kids." She fawns over Andrea's nails and uses magnets to form delicate offsetting lines in her mauve sparkle gel. A pale mauve replaces her pink. They discuss exit paths for Russians dodging the war. Tbilisi may resume flights, but Turkey or Azerbaijan flights remain open. Land crossings north are patrolled.

Lori is not pleased with her pricey massage and the flight left her ankles swollen. Yet her spirits are high. Worried, she asks, "What is up with Missy's face?"

Smiling back she replies, "Diagnosis fillers, black and blue but she'll survive." Missy, needing rest, sits with Lori on sling-back chairs having wine on the Black Sea beach. It's warm, and the dark sea shimmers with the full moon. The moon is so full and round that night, gentle ripples against a war to the far away. The sea's name is foreboding; it is very deep oxygenless at points and the color dark as its name.

The following day all stroll the boardwalk stopping for more Turkish coffee and pastries. The sun is brilliant, and the boardwalk lane of bicycles is busy too. Andrea says, "Let's charter a private boat for a few hours on the sea." They stroll towards the boat docks where eager vendors sell tours by the hour. Andrea sees a young man in his 30s smiling ear to ear. He speaks with just enough fluency in seven languages to arrange rides. Irresistible, Andrea approaches him and negotiates a two-hour tour for three; his name is Rafo, she shares her WhatsApp and explains they will return after lunch in the high tower overlooking the port.

The nearby tower was 426 feet/130 meters high, slowing spins while tourists wine and dine lightly. An open elevator shaft ride to the top is just majestic. She texts Rafo, "We are finished and will be down in 15 minutes, good?"

Rafo: "Very good." He leads them holding their arms to the boat they pile in and enjoy the remaining afternoon. Paying at the end, Rafo mutters, "I am off work at seven."

Andrea: "What time? Seven? That is nice," to herself, Ken Doll?

It is early on the third day and all the ladies load light luggage into the driver's car. Andrea hears a ping and it is Rafo. "Where were you last night?"

Confused, she replies, "Dear, resting and you?"

"Waiting for you," He replies in a clear text.

"Ah, perhaps tonight we can meet for wine, how old are you?"

Rafo: "33."

Andrea warns her cohorts and recommends behavior on vast cultural differences and weather. "Ladies, we will stop for water and eat light. The altitude is high, some roads narrow and roughly paved, cover yourself in dark apparel, no shoulders or legs exposed. Black is good. Many locals will stare at you. Your teeth are very white and scold you if you are in Western apparel for mature ladies. Only a day earlier Missy was told repeatedly by a Middle Eastern tourist 'you whore'." Missy was distressed by the full-cover apparel finding it increasingly uncomfortable to be stared at.

Andrea: "Missy, dear, this is not our country and many neighboring countries visit too! I told you! You're wearing an unacceptable dress and all of us are middle-aged. Also, stray dogs are not cared for well, beg for food, and can carry Rabies. Do not touch them! Do not open and close your purses a lot, no one steals here, but you will drop your passports and credit cards in a canyon ravine. This adventure is like no other, but good walking shoes are necessary for uneven surfaces."

The day trip and tour plans are exhilarating; river rafting; canyon hiking; park walks and shopping, late nights on the beach; mini skyscrapers with 360-degree views from the spinning restaurant. Tourists plazas with Martini in one hand and Saperavi wine in the other. Toasting and recalling our early years, before the wrinkles, bad relationships, and graying hair.

Missy and Lori are pleased with the funk of the seaside city. It's a few days of gallivanting that the underside becomes more visible; the skyscrapers next to failing apartments, unemployed milling about broken streets and sidewalks, many children, corner merchants selling the smallest items and Russia's walking pricey Shih Tzu while strays chase the ducks and hold a post at every restaurant and cafe. The oddities of hailing a taxi, only to be invited to their homes for drinks. Female drivers do not exist. The lack of English and tourist season, with many Middle Eastern visitors; dressed in full black with veils in the heat.

They find there is this infectious happiness amongst the local people no dollar can buy. A spirit and culture are embedded in centuries. The still undeveloped beauty washes over all these faults. In Andrea's heart, she sees a future of westernization and the quirkiness of this country fading. Raff texts her, "I can see you at 9 in the evening."

She replies, "Meet me across the street there is a restaurant bar, there is time to chat then."

Silently, "Why not?"

She texts Nina for backup to check in on her and assist with scheduling room cleaning the following morning, as they will be traveling to tour the canyon for a few days.

Nina replies, "Really? The boat boy?"

Rafo is very shy over wine and polite in providing a consensus for how the evening will advance. "Comfort is all that is needed," Andrea says. They return to her room and continue with a little brandy, he brings protection as she really does not know him. Knowingly, he admits to many lovers. His chest is so hairy, like a forest; his manhood is long and thin. Andrea wants him to penetrate her anus, it's not the pain from London but gentle and welcoming. He asks for his phallus to be suckled. She gladly complies by bobbing and licking his thin long shaft and he releases uncontrollably.

"We should meet again." In his shy manner, he implores Andrea not to embrace him on the street and that the affair be held in secret. She easily agrees as people know them both here. She sleeps soundly, waiting for Ahmed is not enough.

They begin their two-day excursion into the gorges; their young driver is Dato. The low sea plains and marshes line the coast on the way north, stopping for traditional cheese and bean pastries, fresh Turkish coffee cooked in the sand, and a refreshing walk in a controversial park of ancient trees transported by barge and funded by billionaire oligarchs. The air is so very humid and it is hot; the caves are steamy hideaways, but the narrow road to Okatse Canyon and Kinchkha Falls delivers a nail-biting ride to the top to view the cascading water from 85 and from 230 ft. heights. Dato can barely manage the car up the narrow gravel road. Blue water flowing into the river tributaries below and pooling at the basin against yellow chalk cliffs only to again descend another 80 feet. The canyon walls are treacherous for the faint, narrow metal plank ways clinging to the rock walls; exhilarating; agile footings.

Adventurous caves made of limestone and challenging trails for a respite from what is unbearable humidity. The stalactites and stalagmites slowly drip toward each other in cool dim light. At the moment, the roads were so narrow they thought to turn back. The canyon walls are so precarious one feels their knees give way to the smallest wind. A full day, then meeting the tour driver and planning the night for dinner in the village cottages.

The villagers watch the daring few, playing dominoes and drinking local moonshine as they gaze indirectly. Ahmed Whatsapps Andrea, "Dear, all are invited to dinner this evening in the village."

Andrea replies nervously, "Wonderful, we will come, we are very hungry." Ahmed had been resting in the canyon village, she would see him soon, and his nephew would join their tour driver.

Andrea, resting during the return drive. She ponders what it will be like to see Ahmed, but her eyes close, thinking of the steps that led to this very day and ride through the canyons. Missy and Lori feel like they returned to college, free and wild.

Vividly, Andrea recollects the first time she met Missy knocking on her door at college. Groggy, her sparkling blue eyes, smile with straight white teeth in unison, shoulder length bright blond hair, permed like Peter Frampton. Thin and tall. Slurring in a whisper, "It's 2 am, and I am locked out, can I stay with you?" You could smell the beer and see the slight tilt in her posture.

"Sure, I am Andrea, please, come in." They have similar mothers, so the bond was immediate; two mischievous ladies on a trek to experience life. Galway of West Ireland, the beaches of the South, the Italian Alps, the ski slopes of the Northeast. Boys and boys, Missy, a man magnet; Andrea, cute like Annette Funicello, Missy, Cheryl Tiegs, or Christie Brinkley but a soul so deep and heart so warm. A lifetime of trust, with irreplaceable memories, friends, and confidants. She leads a subdued life past the early years. She is a confidant and knows of Ahmed.

Lori, Andrea met her on a double date in high school; a straight, dark-haired beauty and brown eyes. Andrea had a bad boy Ken doll, Mitch and a bad lover, likely due to youth and experience, but this boy was bad to the core. He was not a local, but rather a New York City transfer in her local town making him alluring; bright blue eyes, huge curly red hair, and a full matching beard. Hyperactive and business-minded; a mover of secondhand market goods as played by Morgan Freeman's, *Red* in the 1994 film *Shawshank Redemption*. The local source for white kids' weed and sports equipment. Always money to play, athletic and bubbling. Yet a selfish, hot mess. On this date, Mitch's childhood buddy Chad, Andrea, and Lori met. Chad was a brown-eyed hunk with dark brown ringlet hair that bounced when he spoke. Yes, slight but a hunk, quietly intellectual. Lori, Andrea, Mitch, and Chad, a day filled with traipsing through Manhattan on senior skip day, visiting the Metropolitan Museum of Art, riding the Staten Island ferry, and all-you-can-drink beer joints. Customers buy a burger with fries. Fond day innocence and making out on public benches.

Mitch eventually goes bald and keeps the same sales job for 40 years after smashing his Maserati in the 2008 stock crash. Apparently, he recovered and was last year seen at a Chalet in France. Chad escapes to the mountains of Montana; opens a business and raises a family, now a white-haired hunk as fit as a teenager on Facebook. Lori becomes her long-time friend. She and Lori both return to Midtown Manhattan to relive some of those memories long ago. Only on Facebook does Chad follow his old lady pals to reconnect, with a thumbs up or heart with a comment. Chad ended his friendship with Mitch around the same time as Andrea; a hot mess from 40 years ago. Double thumbs up when seen traveling together. Andrea has Montana on her bucket list and dreamt of adding this Ken doll more than once.

Chapter 6
Dinner

The ride ended, Andrea woke up and they settled in the cottage with peach and hazelnut trees shading the garden. The ladies take in the air and scents. "No worries ladies, you can simply take the peach and eat it, no angry Americans are with us," Ahmed says, "Soon, we will all have dinner."

Andrea replies, "Get it ready in about 30 minutes, please."

Andrea preens and primps. A simple flowing black kerchief dress, offsetting a thin crystal belt, a comfortable slip-on. Eyeliner, cream-colored shadow, her skin is sun-kissed, a light pale pink lipstick, and a few spritzes of Shalimar. Her cohorts are not ready. She rests on the balcony with Ahmed's pistachios. Seeing a deck of cards on the cafe table, she begins to dole out the cards for solitaire, then hears the familiar smoky raspy voice. Below the balcony in the garden, she sees Ahmed chatting with other dinner guests. Beckoning she says, "Hello, Ahmed!"

Cautiously, they smile as he ascends the steps, embracing her. All join them; his nephew, Dato the driver, then Missy and Lori. Gingerly dancing with some small talk, sharing greetings, and introductions. His nephew Kafu chimes in how he is not fond of America, Andrea enjoys his point of view and the similarities with Ahmed and the possibilities of his youth. Kafu is a pharmacist.

Returning to the garden patio they eat a rich dinner; wine flowing, traditional cha-cha, and toasts to health, God, family, and children. As the wine flows, the voices grow loud and politics starts, each stumbling over the other's conversations. Andrea limits her alcohol by chasing the cha-cha with water or dispensing it discreetly to the ground. She wants to control her thoughts and words.

Cha-cha is a strong pomace brandy made from grape pips, stems, and leaves after the harvest. It is boiled in a makeshift kiln in the fall and filtered with cotton making the once sticky pulp froth crystal clear. A 70% home concoction deep in tradition and claims of medicinal uses adding to longevity. It's traditional and does not replace a good slow scotch on ice for Andrea.

As all of them are leaving, Missy whispers, "Be careful of him."

Ahmed embraces each lady and says he will return to her before they all leave, evening ends. "I made a promise," says Ahmed, "I will bring you honey."

Andrea says, "Okay."

Med texts, "I will come for a few days…"

Andrea asks, "Exactly when?"

Chapter 7
Last Night

Ping! It's Rafo. "How are you?"

Andrea: "Very well."

"You are a friend, right?"

Cautiously she says, "Yes, of course."

"I need your help."

Andrea: "And?"

Rafo: "My brother wishes to get his visa and it is $800 and we are short $400."

Ugh! "Dear, you are not my prostitute." She feels insulted but brazen in a nice way.

"Oh, no no you are my friend?" Andrea thinks to give him $100 and he will go away as so many foreigners do this, income is low and so is savings when there is no income. She explains she is deep in helping others, and has commitments but can part with a small amount.

For fast support, she texts Nina. "You're not going to believe this, what did the boat boy ask for?"

Nina: "A visa and money! You do not learn do you and you're still at it!"

Andrea replies, "He was so sweet."

Andrea gives him the $100 and then another $100, he asks a 3rd time and she puts her foot down.

"Ken dolls," Nina says, "I have two and now a new one."

Andrea advises, "Keep them apart at all costs!"

The trip was nearing the end and there would be one last celebratory dinner. Andrea had not heard from Ahmed and the evening was late and the plane would fly home early morning. She meets her ladies in their rooms and is dressed in red ribbed leggings and a matching print flowing blouse; makeup applied perfectly. They, too, were dressed to be out. All smiling and laughing as if young roommates at school; they exit the hall and hear the raspy voice of Ahmed, they all look up. He had returned from the canyons to his seasonal room on the same floor. He hugs Andrea deeply and kisses her. They ask to have a photo on the balcony and he joins them uninvited; three ladies and Ahmed on the 42nd floor balcony with a view of the Black Sea. Lori asks, "How do you know him and how did you meet?"

Andrea replies quickly, "Lunch in the capital, we both worked in tourism." The night was light wine and food and laughing until it was time for a taxi back to sleep.

Returning to her room and bed, Andrea nestles in, her phone pings, it's Ahmed, "Come to me, only if you want."

She ponders and thinks and replies, "If you want, Ahmed."

"Come up to me." She freshens her makeup, wears a loose skirt, thong, and no bra. His text beckons one more time, "Now, come."

"Okay on the way." Like a youth in the middle of the night, she takes the elevator up, thinking cameras are documenting it all, thinking she will wake her guests; with the Henkel knives in tow.

Arriving, he is showering, she peers in at his nakedness. "Hello." He comes out dressed lightly; closes the curtains, arranges the bed cover, turns on the air conditioner, and turns off the lights. "I know you like this comfort and privacy." He sits upon pillows at the head of the bed. Andrea crawls atop the covers and comes close.

"Ahmed, I love making up, are we making up?"

His voice is hoarse from years of chain-smoking, "Come to me, you are such a bitch and you know it." They embrace so tightly with him muttering "I love to fuck women" and her "I love to have sex" and him "I know."

But Andrea says, "Oh, here are the knives, Henkels, the best, steel forged." Pleased Ahmed fondles each one carefully, touching then running his fingers down the razor edge.

"Did you wish me for all of them?" he says in a deep voice.

"Yes, all, place them on the shelf."

He lifts her shirt and clasps her breast with his lips and then teeth and suckles them deeply, then harder biting and nibbling them inflicting light pain. She serves him her other breast. He gorges his mouth on her nipple teething, sucking, and swapping each breast. Then kisses her deeply, only to lower his pants and move her head to his engorged penis to suck him, lick him and pet his sack. He indicates to her to slow down and withdraw his manhood. Lifts her skirt and spreads her legs, buries his head between to suckle her clit.

He mutters, "You bitch," and begins to bite her inner thigh, she writhes in pleasure. He first uses one then two fingers plunging into her vagina, then his whole hand fists her. "You are wet, dear," she mutters back "more". He gives her more, inserting one then two fingers in her anus, she moans. More moans as he deepens his fingers. Her nails are long, she lubricates her fingers and slowly returns the anal satisfaction. Deep into his rectum, he moans in pleasure too. Curly and slightly arching his back with each deeper insertion. She finishes him off with her riding him like a stallion until he spasms. He completes her by rubbing her and fingering her to climax.

He lights a cigarette. She leaves satisfied. "You will be so missed and yes count me in on the cottages. Making up is wonderful," Ahmed says, "I love to fuck women, we've done everything but fuck your ass."

She acknowledges, "No, not yet. Ahmed, I never ask for gifts, please consider the smallest memory a gift for me."

A ping, it's Rafo. "Where are you?"

"Me? I'm in room 223 with friends and busy." There is a knock on the door and it is Rafo, looking for Andrea and more money. Defensively, Ahmed rushes to the door knife in hand, and points it at his throat. Uncontrolled, he runs the blade slicing missing his juggler.

"Don't hurt him," Andrea says. He withdraws the threat and Rafo runs holding his throat.

Andrea's phone pings, it's Med now, she had totally forgotten. "I need to cancel," Andrea texts.

"No problem, love," Med replies, "I love you."

She quickly types, "Me too."

Relieved. It is very late, there is ample time to sleep on the flight. On check-in, with only a few hours of sleep, Andrea receives a complimentary First Class Upgrade. Feeling blessed, she boards with her ladies and returns in luxury.

Chapter 8
Cottages

Andrea arrives stateside and Florida respite is planned as winter is setting in and the cusp of snowbird season, before the Thanksgiving holiday. No Ken dolls in Florida. Andrea enjoys this rest in the temperate weather, having more private time to respond to the texts from Ahmed, writing in peace, and visiting with more lady friends. She is not far from the ocean taking days of warm sun in and mesmerized by the azure crashing waves.

Ahmed, "So are you in? We are close to buying the land?"

Ahmed: "Andrea dear, why not video chat so many months have passed." Her camera and phone ring. She grabs a beer and retreats to her bedroom to speak. The conversation runs for hours till the wee mornings for the other corner of the world.

"You are so happy and never complain."

"Yes, it's just not how God made me dear, but very much a pain in the ass on details." Grabbing another beer and another, Andrea knows that the attention is fulfilling and loves the long chatter. "I can give you this life that you don't have." Andrea knows it is a dream, but she loves the possibility of days of only the sounds of nature and simple life. Her hair can turn gray, her nails unpolished and days spent just caring for her simple needs. Drunk from the beer and attention, she cannot help but smile and laugh and agrees to spend $25,000. Pleased, she arranged a new air ticket. "Let's spend more time like this together."

Ahmed: "It's very late here and time for sleep."

"Goodnight…"

She arranges a money wire to receive in small amounts and on arrival can see how things progress. She forgets about the cruelty and the misogynistic tendencies, for now. With only nuts in her luggage, she is eager to re-board. However, there has been not a single video call after that time and she is getting wary.

Andrea is familiar with neglect, at least she has a dream for a moment. Nina prepares receipts. Many videos are received showing the progress of the cottages, one for her and one for Andrea. The frame, interiors, and flooring are bright hardwood, steel laminated framed, insulated steel roofing, and floors supported on short lallies. Windows framed in matching steel to maximize views as the structures sit at the top of a hill, facing west-east. Looking out over a rolling valley of farms and cascading mountains in the distance. Humid year-round fruit trees are plentiful and gardens of herbs will be planted. Decking for sipping morning coffee and rustic walnut furniture is planned.

Andrea arrives the following spring and with inclement weather, a week passes before traveling north with Nina to visit the cottages.

Andrea did very little manual work as a guest and an investor, which drove her nuts, she likes to get dirty and build with the men, not just sit pretty. And enjoys a hard roll after a long day. The cottages are not ready so they all stay in the other cottages from a few summers back. Andrea alone and Keti share with Ahmed. She thinks little of this; there is no money for private quarters for her and it's best to assume sex with him is possible. Often you see her tapping and slapping him, a sign of want in America.

Another day passes as the weather is inclement. It was the very yellow house that she and Ahmed had a tryst in the middle of the night with sultry muffled moans to not wake the neighbors.

Ahmed walks the property perimeter, then the property below it indicating this land would be next to build a lake for fish and plant the garden. He gestures to fences that need mending and it is good luck the brook runs parallel to the property for water. Then points up towards the electric pole, access has been brought in from the street and all the canalization for the sewer is complete. As if a young man he pulls her hand into his for a moment. She allows the touch. They are near the tall A-frame cottage, which provides cover from the workmen's and other neighbors' eyes. Aggressively, he pulls her toward him for a kiss and squeezes her breast. Andrea says, "Dear, don't get me going, people will see in the village you know this." Before returning to the front for late lunch and still hidden, discussing future plans she says, "Come near me." She kisses him back deeply and gently clenches his groin.

The wooden shed structure was their eating place; dilapidated side walls, disheveled work materials, dirt floor, cows mooing in the background, peeled back card table, tiny chairs of wood that shake, one propane gas burner self-contained, a strung wire for the light bulb and tea kettle. A mix of chipped glasses and pottery, a spigot, and a bucket outside to wash with soap, and a washbasin behind it. A most delicious pork stew in the most delectable spicy pepper tomato sauce. Boiled for hours till it fell off the bone and a pile of local flatbread freshly baked. She was taught language on her many visits and easily stumbled through conversations, but it gets easier after a few shots of cha-cha. Nina was with them the whole day; negotiating with the locals and not engaging in robust meal conversations.

Approaching sunset; Andrea sets her GPS to be able to return to the same cottage location. Andrea notes cottages rise from the hills to the left. The last 200 meters are dirt and would need paving. It was all splendid. She shares the GPS marker with Nina.

Nina will go on to visit other homes with our driver. Andrea declines and surprisingly so does Ahmed. Only they return and there are a few hours of privacy. Both drunk, he visits Andrea promptly, awkward but satisfying. She closes her door and unzips his pants, loosening his bulge and dropping his jeans to the floor, kneeling as she applies stimulating licks, sucks, and takes in his staff. Drunkenly, he pushes her to the bed, she removes her clothing, and with her legs spread he makes love to her and her to him. She begs for ass play and he obeys, then patiently fondles her till climax. He then masturbates as she plays with her breasts and releases all on her. "They will return soon, you should shower."

Chapter 9
Ghosted

The morning comes and a chime of Andrea's phone from Ahmed wakes her up. "Look, seriously since you came you fucked everyone's brain. I will find a way to give your money back. Get rid of this headache." Culturally confused and used. Her anger grows and losing is not an option.

Not regretting her decision to invest in the cottages. She texts back, "No!" Ahmed, does Nina work for you? Does she owe you anything?" Silent, Andrea internalizes; the village must know, Nina must know that's why they left them alone. A shame she did not understand. An American empowered woman in a man's world. Sit pretty and shut up, no advice over a man's word. Play only in the dark.

Repeating in her mind what she said about the cottages and dinner. She had GPS mapped the cottage location. Rambling to herself, Nina always seems to be in the loop. Then receives a text from Nina, never mentioning Ahmed. "If you do not want to be part of us, you should not."

Andrea replies, offended, "Threats of quitting are the most insulting." Nina, "Do not give advice. He will not cheat you, I deeply apologize for the offense as a friend."

Nina's manner and Andrea's endless detailed opinions on the project made her more confused. Other than supplying money, her ideas were clearly unwanted; her ass is on call. Promises were made and it's not past 60% complete. She had been offering ideas in American style. "You are not the boss. You will wait!" blurted Ahmed.

Trying to calm down, she recalls earlier words of Nina, "He always wins," but Andrea likes to win and lives for freedom.

Returning to her memories that made her strong; feelings of rejection. All reminding her of who she is and where the Ken dolls belong.

Anonymous: "He threw me down the stairs, drunk. He came in late and wanted some ass. Stitches later, I am okay."

Another: "Drunk, he tied me to a chair like a dog, seven months pregnant with only water. One day in prison he served and after my brain surgery from the beating, the loan is still being paid at high interest. I don't know what I did and I am still with him."

Another: "He raped me the first day of college, I don't know what I did."

Another: "Returning from class, it was daylight, he followed me to the apartment front door, threatened me to shut up. I went to the neighbor's apartment instead, he clocked my eye and left."

Another: "He raped me it was just a date."

Another: "We were high on coke and liquor, and he threw me to the floor, slamming my head repeatedly, choking my throat giving me what I deserved and loved repeating it."

A dismissive ER attendant said, "Only Hysteria, all is fine." Oddly, John Lennon died that night.

Another: "Fix this young woman's fingertip in his hand, drunk, they place it in milk and she is sent to the ER." Another: "He beat her so bad, she was found in a cemetery dead from an uncontested hotshot suicide, she was a nurse." Another: "The first husband broke her arm, the second her jaw in two places, wiring it shut for three months. She talked too much."

Andrea is wild with fear and comes out of her thoughts. Recalling Ahmed's words, "I like to drink, it makes me happy, you need to know your place." She begins to sweat despite the cold, turns in the blankets restless and phone in hand, thinking to text, then think better of it so she does not. In a foreign country, high in the mountains with only her befriended Nina and enraged Ahmed. All others are strangers, in a culture where women's rights hold up entry to the EU. Trying to control her increasing anxiety, she comes out of hiding to make breakfast in the cottage-shared kitchens. She is greeted by Juva, the patron who runs the small cottages with his wife. He had built them by hand.

Juva has a scruffy beard, and a heavy belly from drinking. He wishes to chat with her, his Georgian look and manners are classic. His English is poor or pretends to be poor, taking out a book for translation. Andrea has seen this pocket black covered book before; with the tiniest print. Her eyesight has started to fail, cataracts in one eye, and she excuses herself to get her readers. Returning and cooking eggs she offers him some. He offers her kiwi fruit still fresh from last season. From a bowl on the table, slowly peeling the skins and slicing. He placed a few pieces on a plate; very sweet and so seemed he. Then he offers a toast of whiskey, and she accepts, it relaxes her, then both toast and they fill and toss back the second, smiling. He motions to pour the third! Giggling, she says, "Two is enough!"

He says, "You are so beautiful." In perfect English. She allows the third fill and both toss it back.

The village life is hard and his wife looks nearly 80, only a year different in age from the traveler. Her anxiety quelled only the first moment from her intoxication. "Thank you," she says with a slipperier slur.

"You are really beautiful." Her morning has been a whirl and the conversation is going sideways. He reaches for her hand, begins to rub it, then touches her knee wanting to refill her glass.

She sees the liquor is low and mumbles, "Sure, let's finish and have a fourth!" He tops her glasses and chugs them down. He reaches again, she says today we will go, thanks him and leaves. Continually reminded men have these patriarchal rights. He offers to return with a fresh liter. Sober enough, she returns to her room and texts Ahmed. "I am drunk, Juva was all over me!"

Ahmed: "You are drunk, he'll drink with anyone. You are a big girl." Extreme anxiety set in, the liquor stirs in her stomach and she vomits.

She and Nina are placed on the local bus 45 minutes from the cottages. It would be a two-and-a-half-hour ride with no heat and it was rainy. Her boots were left out on the stoop; she put plastic bags on her feet to hold back the dampness. Thankfully, a friend meets up roadside and takes them both to the resort on the way. Andrea shoots off a text to Med, "I am back, come to me. I'll pay for the ticket." He agrees.

No word from Ahmed for weeks. He said to wait and she was fearful. Ghosted.

Chapter 10
The Dream

Nina and Andrea return to her room and share some tea. She talks about her dream of a sex room hideaway. A room with flowing sheer veils on tall posts and a selection of bondage choices for clients. Couples can act out fantasies. Swings from the ceiling and suspended sling chairs hanging against the walls to suspend the lady high so her legs can part. Nasty lingerie with nipple holes. Ropes to bind hands and cuffs to ankles. Vibrators and now butt stimulators. For all to orgasm all night like she does. She is not allowed, but it's her dream to provide this for couples on the black web. They giggle endlessly, Andrea thinks it's too dangerous, but they giggle anyway searching for toys on the internet. She has connections with millions of followers to advertise this. Dreams of buying more land and making more cottages. Dreams.

She shares that Med will visit in a few days and asks, "The following day can you have the room cleaned?"

Nina asks if she can meet him.

"Sure, if we come out of the room."

Nina says, "I will leave Ahmed's gift of honey at the door."